# Black Be

## Young Folks' Edition

### By

### Anna Sewell

# Contents

Chapter I My Early Home ............................................................ 1

Chapter II The Hunt .................................................................... 4

Chapter III My Breaking In ......................................................... 8

Chapter IV Birtwick Park .......................................................... 12

Chapter V A Fair Start .............................................................. 15

Chapter VI Merrylegs ............................................................... 20

Chapter VII Going For The Doctor ........................................... 23

Chapter VIII The Parting .......................................................... 27

Chapter IX Earlshall ................................................................. 30

Chapter X A Strike For Liberty ................................................ 35

Chapter XI A Horse Fair .......................................................... 39

Chapter XII A London Cab Horse ............................................ 43

Chapter XIII Dolly And A Real Gentleman .............................. 48

Chapter XIV Poor Ginger ......................................................... 53

Chapter XV ............................................................................... 56

Chapter XVI My Last Home ..................................................... 59

Black Beauty Young Folks' Edition

### Chapter I My Early Home

The first place that I can well remember was a pleasant meadow with a pond of clear water in it. Over the hedge on one side we looked into a plowed field, and on the other we looked over a gate at our them, and had great fun; we used to gallop all together round the field, as hard as we could go. Sometimes we had rather rough play, for they would bite and kick, as well as gallop.

## Anna Sewell

One day, when there was a good deal of kicking, my mother whinnied to me to come to her, and then she said: "I wish you to pay attention to what I am going to say. The colts who live here are very good colts, but they are cart-horse colts, and they have not learned manners. You have been well-bred and well-born; your father has a great name in these parts, and your grandfather won the cup at the races; your grandmother had the sweetest temper of any horse I ever knew, and I think you have never seen me kick or bite. I hope you will grow up gentle and good, and never learn bad ways; do your work with a good will, lift your feet up well when you trot, and never bite or kick even in play."

I have never forgotten my mother's advice. I knew she was a wise old horse, and our master thought a great deal of her. Her name was Duchess, but he called her Pet.

Our master was a good, kind man. He gave us good food, good lodging and kind words; he spoke as kindly to us as he did to his little children. We were all fond of him, and my mother loved him very much. When she saw him at the gate she would neigh with joy, and trot up to him. He would pat and stroke her and say, "Well, old Pet, and how is your little Darkie?" I was a dull black, so he called me

Darkie; then he would give me a piece of bread, which was very good, and sometimes he brought a carrot for my mother. All the horses would come to him, but I think we were his favorites. My mother always took him to town on a market-day in a light gig.

We had a ploughboy, Dick, who sometimes came into our field to pluck blackberries from the hedge. When he had eaten all he wanted he would have what he called fun with the colts, throwing stones and sticks at them to make them gallop. We did not much mind him, for we could gallop off; but sometimes a stone would hit and hurt us.

One day he was at this game, and did not know that the master was in the next field, watching what was going on; over the hedge he jumped in a snap, and catching Dick by the arm, he gave him such a box on the ear as made him roar with the pain and surprise. As soon as we saw the master we trotted up nearer to see what went on.

"Bad boy!" he said, "bad boy! to chase the colts. This is not the first time, but it shall be the last. There—take your money and go home; I shall not want you on my farm again." So we never saw Dick any more. Old Daniel, the man who looked after the horses, was just as gentle as our master; so we were well off.

## Chapter II The Hunt

Before I was two years old a circumstance happened which I have never forgotten. It was early in the spring; there had been a little frost in the night, and a light mist still hung over the woods and meadows. I and the other colts were feeding at the lower part of the field when we heard what sounded like the cry of dogs. The oldest of the colts raised his head, pricked his ears, and said, "There are the hounds!" and cantered off, followed by the rest of us, to the upper part of the field, where we could look over the hedge and see several fields beyond. My mother and an old riding horse of our master's were also standing near, and seemed to know all about it. "They have found a hare," said my mother, "and if they come this way we shall see the hunt."

And soon the dogs were all tearing down the field of young wheat next to ours. I never heard such a noise as they made. They did not bark, nor howl, nor whine, but kept on a "yo! yo, o, o! yo, o, o!" at the top of their voices. After them came a number of men on horseback, all galloping as fast as they could. The old horses snorted and looked eagerly after them, and we young colts wanted to be galloping with them, but they were soon away into the fields lower down; here it seemed as if they had come to a stand; the dogs left off barking and ran about every way with their noses to the ground.

"They have lost the scent," said the old horse; "perhaps the hare will get off."

"What hare?" I said.

"Oh, I don't know what hare; likely enough it may be one of our own hares out of the woods; any hare they can find will do for the dogs and men to run after"; and before long the dogs began their "yo; yo, o, o!" again, and back they came all together at full speed, making straight for our meadow at the part where the high bank and hedge overhang the brook.

"Now we shall see the hare," said my mother; and just then a hare, wild with fright, rushed by and made for the woods. On came the dogs; they burst over the bank, leaped the stream and came dashing across the field, followed by the huntsmen. Several men leaped their horses clean over, close upon the dogs. The hare tried to get through the fence; it was too thick, and she turned sharp around to make for the road, but it was too late; the dogs were upon her with their wild cries; we heard one shriek, and that was the end of her. One of the huntsmen rode up and whipped off the dogs, who would soon have torn her to pieces. He held her up by the leg, torn and bleeding, and all the gentlemen seemed well pleased.

As for me, I was so astonished that I did not at first see what was going on by the brook; but when I did look, there was a sad sight; two fine horses were down; one was struggling in the stream, and the other was groaning on the grass. One of the riders was getting out of the water covered with mud, the other lay quite still.

"His neck is broken," said my mother.

"And serves him right, too," said one of the colts.

I thought the same, but my mother did not join with us.

"Well, no," she said, "you must not say that; but though I am an old horse, and have seen and heard a great deal, I never yet could make out why men are so fond of this sport; they often hurt themselves, often spoil good horses, and tear up the fields, and all for a hare, or a fox, or a stag, that they could get more easily some other way; but we are only horses, and don't know."

While my mother was saying this, we stood and looked on. Many of the riders had gone to the young man; but my master was the first to raise him. His head fell back and his arms hung down, and every one looked very serious. There was no noise now; even the dogs were quiet, and seemed to know that something was wrong. They carried him to our master's house. I heard afterwards that it was the squire's only son, a fine, tall young man, and the pride of his family.

They were now riding in all directions—to the doctor's, and to Squire Gordon's, to let him know about his son. When Bond, the farrier, came to look at the black horse that lay groaning on the grass, he felt him all over, and shook his head; one of his legs was broken. Then some one ran to our master's house and came back with a gun; presently there was a loud bang and a dreadful shriek, and then all was still; the black horse moved no more.

My mother seemed much troubled; she said she had known that horse for years, and that his name was Rob Roy; he was a good horse, and there was no vice in him. She never would go to that part of the field afterwards.

Not many days after, we heard the church-bell tolling for a long time, and looking over the gate, we saw a long strange black coach that was covered with black cloth and was drawn by black horses; after that came another and another and another, and all were black, while the bell kept tolling, tolling. They were carrying young Gordon to the church-yard to bury him. He would never ride again. What they did with Rob Roy I never knew; but 'twas all for one little hare.

## Chapter III My Breaking In

I was now beginning to grow handsome, my coat had grown fine and soft, and was bright black. I had one white foot and a pretty white star on my forehead. I was thought very handsome; my master would not sell me till I was four years old; he said lads ought not to work like men, and colts ought not to work like horses till they were quite grown up.

When I was four years old, Squire Gordon came to look at me. He examined my eyes, my mouth, and my legs; he felt them all down, and then I had to walk and trot and gallop before him; he seemed to like me, and said, "When he has been well broken in he will do very well." My master said he would break me in himself, and he lost no time about it, for the next day he began.

Every one may not know what breaking in is, therefore I will describe it. It means to teach a horse to wear a saddle and bridle, and to carry on his back a man, woman, or child; to go just the way they wish, and to go quietly. Besides this, he has to learn to wear a collar, and a breeching, and to stand still while they are put on; then to have a cart or a buggy fixed behind, so that he cannot walk or trot without dragging it after him; and he must go fast or slow, just as his driver wishes. He must never start at what he sees, nor speak to other horses, nor bite, nor kick, nor have any will of his own, but always do his master's will, even though he may be very tired or hungry; but the worst of all is, when his harness is once on, he may neither jump for joy nor lie down for weariness. So you see this breaking in is a great thing.

I had, of course, long been used to a halter and a head-stall, and to be led about in the fields and lanes quietly, but now I was to have a bit and bridle; my master gave me some oats as usual, and after a good deal of coaxing he got the bit into my mouth and the bridle fixed, but it was a nasty thing! Those who have never had a bit in their mouths cannot think how bad it feels; a great piece of cold hard steel as thick as a man's finger to be pushed into one's mouth, between one's teeth, and over one's tongue, with the ends coming out at the corner of your mouth, and held fast there by straps over your head, under your throat, round your nose, and under your chin; so that no way in the world can you get rid of the nasty hard thing; it is very bad! at least I thought so; but I knew my mother always wore one when she went out, and all horses did when they were grown up; and so, what with the nice oats, and what with my master's pats, kind words, and gentle ways, I got to wear my bit and bridle.

Next came the saddle, but that was not half so bad; my master put it on my back very gently, while Old Daniel held my head; he then made the girths fast under my body, patting and talking to me all the time; then I had a few oats, then a little leading about; and this he did every day till I began to look for the oats and the saddle. At length, one morning, my master got on my back and rode me around the meadow on the soft grass. It certainly did feel queer; but I must say I felt rather proud to carry my master, and as he continued to ride me a little every day, I soon became accustomed to it.

The next unpleasant business was putting on the iron shoes; that too was very hard at first. My master went with me to the smith's forge, to see that I was not hurt or got any fright. The blacksmith took my feet in his hand, one after the other, and cut away some of the hoof. It did not pain me, so I stood still on three legs till he had done them all. Then he took a piece of iron the shape of my foot, and clapped it on, and drove some nails through the shoe quite into my hoof, so that the shoe was firmly on. My feet felt very stiff and heavy, but in time I got used to it.

And now having got so far, my master went on to break me to harness; there were more new things to wear. First, a stiff heavy collar just on my neck, and a bridle with great side-pieces against my eyes, called blinkers, and blinkers indeed they were, for I could not see on either side, but only straight in front of me; next there was a small saddle with a nasty stiff strap that went right under my tail; that was the crupper. I hated the crupper—to have my long tail doubled up and poked through that strap was almost as bad as the bit. I never felt more like kicking, but of course I could not kick such a good master, and so in time I got used to everything, and could do my work as well as my mother.

I must not forget to mention one part of my training, which I have always considered a very great advantage. My master sent me for a fortnight to a neighboring farmer's, who had a meadow which was skirted on one side by the railway. Here were some sheep and cows, and I was turned in among them.

I shall never forget the first train that ran by. I was feeding quietly near the pales which separated the meadow from the railway, when I heard a strange sound at a distance, and before I knew whence it came—with a rush and a clatter, and a puffing out of smoke—a long black train of something flew by, and was gone almost before I could draw my breath. I galloped to the further side of the meadow, and there I stood snorting with astonishment and fear. In the course of the day many other trains went by, some more slowly; these drew up at the station close by, and sometimes made an awful shriek and groan before they stopped. I thought it very dreadful, but the cows went on eating very quietly, and hardly raised their heads as the black, frightful thing came puffing and grinding past. For the first few days I could not feed in peace; but as I found that this terrible creature never came into the field, or did me any harm, I began to disregard it, and very soon I cared as little about the passing of a train as the cows and sheep did.

Since then I have seen many horses much alarmed and restive at the sight or sound of a steam engine; but, thanks to my good master's care, I am as fearless at railway stations as in my own stable. Now if any one wants to break in a young horse well, that is the way.

My master often drove me in double harness, with my mother, because she was steady and could teach me how to go better than a strange horse. She told me the better I behaved the better I should be treated, and that it was wisest always to do my best to please my master. "I hope you will fall into good hands, but a horse never knows who may buy him, or who may drive him; it is all a chance for us; but still I say, do your best wherever it is, and keep up your good name."

## Chapter IV Birtwick Park

It was early in May, when there came a man from Gordon's, who took me away to the Hall. My master said, "Good-bye, Darkie; be a good horse and always do your best." I could not say "good-bye," so I put my nose in his hand; he patted me kindly, and I left my first home. I will describe the stable into which I was taken; this was very roomy, with four good stalls; a large swinging window opened into the yard, making it pleasant and airy.

The first stall was a large square one, shut in behind with a wooden gate; the others were common stalls, good stalls, but not nearly so large. It had a low rack for hay and a low manger for corn; it was called a box stall, because the horse that was put into it was not tied up, but left loose, to do as he liked. It is a great thing to have a box stall.

Into this fine box the groom put me; it was clean, sweet, and airy. I never was in a better box than that, and the sides were not so high but that I could see all that went on through the iron rails that were at the top.

He gave me some very nice oats, patted me, spoke kindly, and then went away.

When I had eaten my oats, I looked round. In the stall next to mine stood a little fat gray pony, with a thick mane and tail, a very pretty head, and a pert little nose. I put my head up to the iron rails at the top of my box, and said, "How do you do? What is your name?"

He turned round as far as his halter would allow, held up his head, and said, "My name is Merrylegs. I am very handsome. I carry the young ladies on my back, and sometimes I take our mistress out in the low cart. They think a great deal of me, and so does James. Are you going to live next door to me in the box?"

I said, "Yes."

"Well, then," he said, "I hope you are good-tempered; I do not like any one next door who bites." Just then a horse's head looked over from the stall beyond; the ears were laid back, and the eye looked rather ill-tempered. This was a tall chestnut mare, with a long handsome neck; she looked across to me and said, "So it is you have turned me out of my box; it is a very strange thing for a colt like you to come and turn a lady out of her own home."

"I beg your pardon," I said, "I have turned no one out; the man who brought me put me here, and I had nothing to do with it. I never had words yet with horse or mare, and it is my wish to live at peace."

"Well," she said, "we shall see; of course, I do not want to have words with a young thing like you." I said no more. In the afternoon, when she went out, Merrylegs told me all about it.

"The thing is this," said Merrylegs, "Ginger has a habit of biting and snapping; that is why they call her Ginger, and when she was in the box-stall, she used to snap very much. One day she bit James in the arm and made it bleed, and so Miss Flora and Miss Jessie, who are very fond of me, were afraid to come into the stable. They used to bring me nice things to eat, an apple, or a carrot, or a piece of bread, but after Ginger stood in that box, they dared not come, and I missed them very much. I hope they will now come again, if you do not bite or snap." I told him I never bit anything but grass, hay, and corn, and could not think what pleasure Ginger found it.

"Well, I don't think she does find pleasure," says Merrylegs; "it is just a bad habit; she says no one was ever kind to her, and why should she not bite? Of course, it is a very bad habit; but I am sure, if all she says be true, she must have been very ill-used before she came here. John does all he can to please her; so I think she might be good-tempered here. You see," he said, with a wise look, "I am twelve years old; I know a great deal, and I can tell you there is not a better place for a horse all round the country than this. John is the best groom that ever was; he has been here fourteen years; and you never saw such a kind boy as James is, so that it is all Ginger's own fault that she did not stay in that box."

## Chapter V A Fair Start

The name of the coachman was John Manly; he had a wife and one child, and lived in the coachman's cottage, near the stables.

The next morning he took me into the yard and gave me a good grooming, and just as I was going into my box, with my coat soft and bright, the squire came in to look at me, and seemed pleased. "John," he said, "I meant to have tried the new horse this morning, but I have other business. You may as well take him around after breakfast; go by the common and the Highwood, and back by the water-mill and the river; that will show his paces."

"I will, sir," said John. After breakfast he came and fitted me with a bridle. He was very particular in letting out and taking in the straps, to fit my head comfortably; then he brought a saddle, but it was not broad enough for my back; he saw it in a minute, and went for another, which fitted nicely. He rode me first slowly, then a trot, then a canter, and when we were on the common, he gave me a light touch with his whip, and we had a splendid gallop.

"Ho, ho! my boy," he said, as he pulled me up, "you would like to follow the hounds, I think."

As we came back through the park we met the squire and Mrs. Gordon walking; they stopped, and John jumped off. "Well, John, how does he go?"

"First rate, sir," answered John; "he is as fleet as a deer, and has a fine spirit, too; but the lightest touch of the rein will guide him. Down at the end of the common we met one of those traveling carts hung all over with baskets, rugs, and such like; you know, sir, many horses will not pass those carts quietly; he just took a good look at it, and then went on as quiet and pleasant as could be. They were shooting rabbits near the Highwood, and a gun went off close by; he pulled up a little and looked, but he did not stir a step to right or left. I just held the rein steady and did not hurry him, and it's my opinion he has not been frightened or ill-used while he was young."

"That's well," said the squire, "I will try him myself to-morrow."

The next day I was brought up for my master. I remembered my mother's counsel and my good old master's, and I tried to do exactly what he wanted me to do. I found he was a very good rider, and thoughtful for his horse, too. When he came home, the lady was at the hall door as he rode up. "Well, my dear," she said, "how do you like him?"

"He is exactly what John said," he replied; "a pleasanter creature I never wish to mount. What shall we call him?"

She said: "He is really quite a beauty, and he has such a sweet, good-tempered face and such a fine, intelligent eye—what do you say to calling him 'Black Beauty'?"

"Black Beauty—why, yes, I think that is a very good name. If you like, it shall be his name"; and so it was.

When John went into the stable, he told James that the master and mistress had chosen a good sensible name for me, that meant something. They both laughed, and James said, "If it was not for bringing back the past, I should have named him Rob Roy, for I never saw two horses more alike." "That's no wonder," said John; "didn't you know that Farmer Grey's old Duchess was the mother of them both?"

I had never heard that before; and so poor Rob Roy who was killed at that hunt was my brother! I did not wonder that my mother was so troubled. It seems that horses have no relations; at least they never know each other after they are sold.

John seemed very proud of me; he used to make my mane and tail almost as smooth as a lady's hair, and he would talk to me a great deal; of course, I did not understand all he said, but I learned more and more to know what he meant, and what he wanted me to do. I grew very fond of him, he was so gentle and kind; he seemed to know just how a horse feels, and when he cleaned me he knew the tender places and the ticklish places; when he brushed my head, he went as carefully over my eyes as if they were his own, and never stirred up any ill-temper.

James Howard, the stable boy, was just as gentle and pleasant in his way, so I thought myself well off. There was another man who helped in the yard, but he had very little to do with Ginger and me.

A few days after this I had to go out with Ginger in the carriage. I wondered how we should get on together; but except laying her ears back when I was led up to her, she behaved very well. She did her work honestly, and did her full share, and I never wish to have a better partner in double harness. When we came to a hill, instead of slackening her pace, she would throw her weight right into the collar, and pull away straight up. We had both the same sort of courage at our work, and John had oftener to hold us in than to urge us forward; he never had to use the whip with either of us; then our paces were much the same, and I found it very easy to keep step with her when trotting, which made it pleasant, and master always liked it when we kept step well, and so did John. After we had been out two or three times together we grew quite friendly and sociable, which made me feel very much at home.

As for Merrylegs, he and I soon became great friends; he was such a cheerful, plucky, good-tempered little fellow, that he was a favorite with every one, and especially with Miss Jessie and Flora, who used to ride him about in the orchard, and have fine games with him and their little dog Frisky.

## Chapter VI Merrylegs

Mr. Blomefield, the vicar, had a large family of boys and girls; sometimes they used to come and play with Miss Jessie and Flora. One of the girls was as old as Miss Jessie; two of the boys were older, and there were several little ones. When they came, there was plenty of work for Merrylegs, for nothing pleased them so much as getting on him by turns and riding him all about the orchard and the home paddock, and this they would do by the hour together.

One afternoon he had been sent out with them a long time, and when James brought him in and put on his halter, he said: "There, you rogue, mind how you behave yourself, or we shall get into trouble."

"What have you been doing, Merrylegs?" I asked.

"Oh!" said he, tossing his little head, "I have only been giving those young people a lesson; they did not know when they had enough, so I just pitched them off backwards; that was the only thing they could understand."

"What?" said I, "you threw the children off? I thought you did know better than that! Did you throw Miss Jessie or Miss Flora?"

He looked very much offended, and said: "Of course not; I would not do such a thing for the best oats that ever came into the stable; why, I am as careful of our young ladies as the master could be, and as for the little ones, it is I who teach them to ride. When they seem frightened or a little unsteady on my back, I go as smooth and as quiet as old pussy when she is after a bird; and when they are all right I go on again faster, you see, just to use them to it; so don't you trouble yourself preaching to me; I am the best friend and the best riding-master those children have. It is not them, it is the boys; boys," said he, shaking his mane, "are quite different, they must be broken in, as we were broken in when we were colts, and just be taught what's what. The other children had ridden me about for nearly two hours, and then the boys thought it was their turn, and so it was, and I was quite agreeable. They rode me by turns, and I galloped them about, up and down the fields and all about the orchard, for a good hour. They had each cut a great hazel stick for a riding whip, and laid it on a little too hard; but I took it in good part, till at last I thought we had had enough, so I stopped two or three times by way of a hint. Boys think a horse or pony is like a steam engine, and can go as long and as fast as they please; they never think that a pony can get tired, or have any feelings; so as the one who was whipping me could not understand, I just rose up on my hind legs and let him slip off behind—that was all; he mounted me again, and I did the same. Then the other boy got up, and as soon as he began to use his stick, I laid him on the grass, and so on, till they were able to understand, that was all. They were not bad boys; they don't wish to be cruel. I like them very well; but you see I had to give them a lesson. When they brought me to James and told him, I think he was very angry to see such big sticks. He said they were not for young gentlemen."

"If I had been you," said Ginger, "I would have given those boys a good kick, and that would have given them a lesson."

"No doubt you would," said Merrylegs; "but then I am not quite such a fool as to anger our master or make James ashamed of me; besides, those children are under my charge when they are riding; I tell you they are entrusted to me. Why, only the other day I heard our master say to Mrs. Blomefield, 'My dear madam, you need not be anxious about the children; my old Merrylegs will take as much care of them as you or I could; I assure you I would not sell that pony for any money, he is so perfectly good-tempered and trustworthy'; and do you think I am such an ungrateful brute as to forget all the kind treatment I have had here for five years, and all the trust they place in me, and turn vicious, because a couple of ignorant boys used me badly? No, no! you never had a good place where they were kind to you, and so you don't know, and I am sorry for you; but I can tell you good places make good horses. I wouldn't vex our people for anything; I love them, I do," said Merrylegs, and he gave a low "ho, ho, ho," through his nose, as he used to do in the morning when he heard James' footstep at the door.

## Chapter VII Going For The Doctor

One night I was lying down in my straw fast asleep, when I was suddenly roused by the stable bell ringing very loud. I heard the door of John's house open, and his feet running up to the Hall. He was back again in no time; he unlocked the stable door, and came in, calling out, "Wake up, Beauty! you must go well now, if ever you did"; and almost before I could think, he had got the saddle on my back and the bridle on my head. He just ran around for his coat, and then took me at a quick trot up to the Hall door. The Squire stood there, with a lamp in his hand. "Now, John," he said, "ride for your life—that is, for your mistress' life; there is not a moment to lose. Give this note to Dr. White; give your horse a rest at the inn, and be back as soon as you can."

John said, "Yes, sir," and was on my back in a minute. The gardener who lived at the lodge had heard the bell ring, and was ready with the gate open, and away we went through the park, and through the village, and down the hill till we came to the toll-gate. John called very loud and thumped upon the door; the man was soon out and flung open the gate.

"Now," said John, "do you keep the gate open for the doctor; here's the money," and off we went again.

Anna Sewell

There was before us a long piece of level road by the river-side; John said to me, "Now, Beauty, do your best," and so I did; I wanted no whip nor spur, and for two miles I galloped as fast I could lay my feet to the ground; I don't believe that my old grandfather, who won the race at Newmarket, could have gone faster. When we came to the bridge, John pulled me up a little and patted my neck. "Well done, Beauty! good old fellow," he said. He would have let me go slower, but my spirit was up, and I was off again as fast as before. The air was frosty, the moon was bright; it was very pleasant. We came through a village, then through a dark wood, then uphill, then downhill, till after an eight miles' run, we came to the town, through the streets and into the market-place. It was all quite still except the clatter of my feet on the stones—everybody was asleep. The church clock struck three as we drew up at Dr. White's door. John rang the bell twice, and then knocked at the door like thunder. A window was thrown up, and the doctor, in his night-cap, put his head out and said, "What do you want?"

"Mrs. Gordon is very ill, sir; master wants you to go at once; he thinks she will die if you cannot get there. Here is a note."

"Wait," he said, "I will come."

He shut the window and was soon at the door. "The worst of it is," he said, "that my horse has been out all day, and is quite done up; my son has just been sent for, and he has taken the other. What is to be done? Can I have your horse?"

"He has come at a gallop nearly all the way, sir, and I was to give him a rest here; but I think my master would not be against it, if you think fit, sir."

"All right," he said; "I will soon be ready."

John stood by me and stroked my neck. I was very hot. The doctor came out with his riding-whip. "You need not take that, sir," said John; "Black Beauty will go till he drops. Take care of him, sir, if you can; I should not like any harm to come to him."

"No, no, John," said the doctor, "I hope not," and in a minute we had left John far behind.

I will not tell about our way back. The doctor was a heavier man than John, and not so good a rider; however, I did my very best. The man at the toll-gate had it open. When we came to the hill, the doctor drew me up. "Now, my good fellow," he said, "take some breath." I was glad he did, for I was nearly spent, but that breathing helped me on, and soon we were in the park. Joe was at the lodge gate; my master was at the Hall door, for he had heard us coming. He spoke not a word; the doctor went into the house with him, and Joe led me to the stable. I was glad to get home; my legs shook under me, and I could only stand and pant. I had not a dry hair on my body, the water ran down my legs, and I steamed all over—Joe used to say, like a pot on the fire. Poor Joe! he was young and small, and as yet he knew very little, and his father, who would have helped him, had been sent to the next village; but I am sure he did the very best he knew. He rubbed my legs and my chest, but he did not put my warm cloth on me; he thought I was so hot I should not like it. Then he gave me a pail full of water to drink; it was cold and very good, and I drank it all; then he gave me some hay and some corn, and, thinking he had done right, he went away. Soon I began to shake and tremble, and turned deadly cold; my legs ached, my loins ached, and my chest ached, and I felt sore all over. This developed into a strong inflammation, and I could not draw my breath without pain. John nursed me night and day. My master, too, often came to see me. "My poor Beauty," he said one day, "my good horse, you saved your mistress' life, Beauty; yes, you saved her life." I was very glad to hear that, for it seems the doctor had said if we had been a little longer it would have been too late. John told my master he never saw a horse go so fast in his life. It seems as if the horse knew what was the matter. Of course I did, though John thought not; at least I knew as much as this—that John and I must go at the top of our speed, and that it was for the sake of the mistress.

## Chapter VIII The Parting

I had lived in this happy place three years, but sad changes were about to come over us. We heard that our mistress was ill. The doctor was often at the house, and the master looked grave and anxious. Then we heard that she must go to a warm country for two or three years. The news fell upon the household like the tolling of a death-bell. Everybody was sorry. The master arranged for breaking up his establishment and leaving England. We used to hear it talked about in our stable; indeed, nothing else was talked about. John went about his work silent and sad, and Joe scarcely whistled. There was a great deal of coming and going; Ginger and I had full work.

The first of the party who went were Miss Jessie and Flora with their governess. They came to bid us good-bye. They hugged poor Merrylegs like an old friend, and so indeed he was. Then we heard what had been arranged for us. Master had sold Ginger and me to an old friend. Merrylegs he had given to the vicar, who was wanting a pony for Mrs. Blomefield, but it was on the condition that he should never be sold, and that when he was past work he should be shot and buried. Joe was engaged to take care of him and to help in the house, so I thought that Merrylegs was well off.

"Have you decided what to do, John?" he said.

"No, sir; I have made up my mind that if I could get a situation with some first-rate colt-breaker and horse-trainer, it would be the right thing for me. Many young animals are frightened and spoiled by wrong treatment, which need not be if the right man took them in hand. I always get on well with horses, and if I could help some of them to a fair start I should feel as if I was doing some good. What do you think of it, sir?"

"I don't know a man anywhere," said master, "that I should think so suitable for it as yourself. You understand horses, and somehow they understand you, and I think you could not do better."

The last sad day had come; the footman and the heavy luggage had gone off the day before, and there were only master and mistress, and her maid. Ginger and I brought the carriage up to the Hall door, for the last time. The servants brought out cushions and rugs, and when all were arranged, master came down the steps carrying the mistress in his arms (I was on the side next the house, and could see all that went on); he placed her carefully in the carriage, while the house servants stood round crying.

"Good-bye, again," he said; "we shall not forget any of you," and he got in. "Drive on, John." Joe jumped up and we trotted slowly through the park and through the village, where the people were standing at their doors to have a last look and to say, "God bless them."

When we reached the railway station, I think mistress walked from the carriage to the waiting-room. I heard her say in her own sweet voice, "Good-bye, John; God bless you." I felt the rein twitch, but John made no answer; perhaps he could not speak. As soon as Joe had taken the things out of the carriage, John called him to stand by the horses, while he went on the platform. Poor Joe! He stood close up to our heads to hide his tears. Very soon the train came puffing into the station; then two or three minutes, and the doors were slammed to; the guard whistled and the train glided away, leaving behind it only clouds of white smoke and some very heavy hearts.

When it was quite out of sight, John came back. "We shall never see her again," he said—"never." He took the reins, mounted the box, and with Joe drove slowly home; but it was not our home now.

## Chapter IX Earlshall

The next morning after breakfast, Joe put Merrylegs into the mistress' low chaise to take him to the vicarage; he came first and said good-bye to us, and Merrylegs neighed to us from the yard. Then John put the saddle on Ginger and the leading rein on me, and rode us across the country to Earlshall Park, where the Earl of W---- lived. There was a very fine house and a great deal of stabling. We went into the yard through a stone gateway, and John asked for Mr. York. It was some time before he came. He was a fine-looking, middle-aged man, and his voice said at once that he expected to be obeyed. He was very friendly and polite to John, and after giving us a slight look, he called a groom to take us to our boxes, and invited John to take some refreshment.

We were taken to a light, airy stable, and placed in boxes adjoining each other, where we were rubbed down and fed. In about half an hour John and York, who was to be our new coachman, came in to see us.

"Now, Manly," he said, after carefully looking at us both, "I can see no fault in these horses; but we all know that horses have their peculiarities as well as men, and that sometimes they need different treatment. I should like to know if there is anything particular in either of these that you would like to mention."

"Well," said John, "I don't believe there is a better pair of horses in the country, and right grieved I am to part with them, but they are not alike. The black one is the most perfect temper I ever knew; I suppose he has never known a hard word or blow since he was foaled, and all his pleasure seems to be to do what you wish; but the chestnut, I fancy, must have had bad treatment; we heard as much from the dealer. She came to us snappish and suspicious, but when she found what sort of place ours was, it all went off by degrees; for three years I have never seen the smallest sign of temper, and if she is well treated there is not a better, more willing animal than she is. But she has naturally a more irritable constitution than the black horse; flies tease her more; anything wrong in her harness frets her more; and if she were ill-used or unfairly treated she would not be unlikely to give tit for tat. You know that many high-mettled horses will do so."

"Of course," said York, "I quite understand; but you know it is not easy in stables like these to have all the grooms just what they should be. I do my best, and there I must leave it. I'll remember what you have said about the mare." They were going out of the stable, when John stopped, and said, "I had better mention that we have never used the check-rein with either of them; the black horse never had one on, and the dealer said it was the gag-bit that spoiled the other's temper."

"Well," said York, "if they come here, they must wear the check-rein. I prefer a loose rein myself, and his lordship is always very reasonable about horses; but my lady—that's another thing; she will have style, and if her carriage horses are not reined up tight she wouldn't look at them. I always stand out against the gag-bit, and shall do so, but it must be tight up when my lady rides!"

"I am sorry for it," said John; "but I must go now, or I shall lose the train."

He came round to each of us to pat and speak to us for the last time; his voice sounded very sad. I held my face close to him; that was all I could do to say good-bye; and then he was gone, and I have never seen him since.

The next day Lord W---- came to look at us; he seemed pleased with our appearance. "I have great confidence in these horses," he said, "from the character my friend Gordon has given me of them. Of course they are not a match in color, but my idea is that they will do very well for the carriage while we are in the country. Before we go to London I must try to match Baron; the black horse, I believe, is perfect for riding."

York then told him what John had said about us.

"Well," said he, "you must keep an eye to the mare, and put the check-rein easy; I dare say they will do very well with a little humoring at first. I'll mention it to your lady."

In the afternoon we were harnessed and put in the carriage and led round to the front of the house. It was all very grand, and three times as large as the old house at Birtwick, but not half so pleasant, if a horse may have an opinion. Two footmen were standing ready,, dressed in drab livery, with scarlet breeches and white stockings. Presently we heard the rustling sound of silk as my lady came down the flight of stone steps. She stepped round to look at us; she was a tall, proud-looking woman, and did not seem pleased about something, but she said nothing, and got into the carriage. This was the first time of wearing a check-rein, and I must say, though it certainly was a nuisance not to be able to get my head down now and then, it did not pull my head higher than I was accustomed to carry it. I felt anxious about Ginger, but she seemed to be quiet and content.

Black Beauty Young Folks' Edition

The next day we were again at the door, and the footmen as before; we heard the silk dress rustle, and the lady came down the steps, and in an imperious voice, she said, "York, you must put those horses' heads higher, they are not fit to be seen."

York got down, and said very respectfully, "I beg your pardon, my lady, but these horses have not been reined up for three years, and my lord said it would be safer to bring them to it by degrees; but, if your ladyship pleases, I can take them up a little more." ˛ "Do so," she said.

York came round to our heads and shortened the rein himself, one hole, I think. Every little makes a difference, be it for better or worse, and that day we had a steep hill to go up. Then I began to understand what I had heard of. Of course, I wanted to put my head forward and take the carriage up with a will as we had been used to do; but no, I had to pull with my head up now, and that took all the spirit out of me, and the strain came on my back and legs. When we came in, Ginger said, "Now you see what it is like; but this is not bad, and if it does not get much worse than this I shall say nothing about it, for we are very well treated here; but if they strain me up tight, why, let 'em look out! I can't bear it, and I won't."

Day by day, hole by hole, our bearing-reins were shortened, and instead of looking forward with pleasure to having my harness put on, as I used to do, I began to dread it. Ginger too seemed restless, thought she said very little. The worst was yet to come.

## Chapter X A Strike For Liberty

One day my lady came down later than usual, and the silk rustled more than ever. "Drive to the Duchess of B----'s," she said, and then after a pause, "Are you never going to get those horses' heads up, York? Raise them at once, and let us have no more of this humoring nonsense."

York came to me first, while the groom stood at Ginger's head. He drew my head back and fixed the rein so tight that it was almost intolerable; then he went to Ginger, who was impatiently jerking her head up and down against the bit, as was her way now. She had a good idea of what was coming, and the moment York took the rein off the turret in order to shorten it, she took her opportunity, and reared up so suddenly that York had his nose roughly hit and his hat knocked off; the groom was nearly thrown off his legs. At once they both flew to her head, but she was a match for them, and went on plunging, rearing, and kicking in a most desperate manner; at last she kicked right over the carriage pole and fell down, after giving me a severe blow on my near quarter. There is no knowing what further mischief she might have done, had not York sat himself down flat on her head to prevent her struggling, at the same time calling out, "Unbuckle the black horse! Run for the winch and unscrew the carriage pole! Cut the trace here, somebody, if you can't unhitch it!" The groom soon set me free from Ginger and the carriage, and led me to my box. He just turned me in as I was, and ran back to York. I was much excited by what had happened, and if I had ever been used to kick or rear I am sure I should have done it then; but I never had, and there I stood, angry, sore in my leg, my head still strained up to the terret on the saddle, and no power to get it down. I was very miserable, and felt much inclined to kick the first person who came near me.

Before long, however, Ginger was led in by two grooms, a good deal knocked about and bruised. York came with her and gave us orders, and then came to look at me. In a moment he let down my head.

"Confound these check-reins!" he said to himself; "I thought we should have some mischief soon. Master will be sorely vexed. But here, if a woman's husband can't rule her, of course a servant can't; so I wash my hands of it, and if she can't get to the Duchess' garden party I can't help it."

York did not say this before the men; he always spoke respectfully when they were by. Now he felt me all over, and soon found the place above my hock where I had been kicked. It was swelled and painful; he ordered it to be sponged with hot water, and then some lotion was put on.

Lord W--- was much put out when he learned what had happened; he blamed York for giving way to his mistress, to which he replied that in future he would much prefer to receive his orders only from his lordship. I thought York might have stood up better for his horses, but perhaps I am no judge.

Ginger was never put into the carriage again, but when she was well of her bruises one of Lord W----'s younger sons said he should like to have her; he was sure she would make a good hunter. As for me, I was obliged still to go in the carriage, and had a fresh partner called Max; he had always been used to the tight rein. I asked him how it was he bore it.

"Well," he said, "I bear it because I must; but it is shortening my life, and it will shorten yours too, if you have to stick to it."

"Do you think," I said, "that our masters know how bad it is for us?"

"I can't say," he replied, "but the dealers and the horse-doctors know it very well. I was at a dealer's once, who was training me and another horse to go as a pair; he was getting our heads up, and he said, a little higher and a little higher every day. A gentleman who was there asked him why he did so. 'Because,' said he, 'people won't buy them unless we do. The fashionable people want their horses to carry their heads high and to step high. Of course, it is very bad for the horses, but then it is good for trade. The horses soon wear up, and they come for another pair.' That," said Max, "is what he said in my hearing, and you can judge for yourself."

What I suffered with that rein for four months in my lady's carriage would be hard to describe; but I am quite sure that, had it lasted much longer, either my health or my temper would have, given way. Before that, I never knew what it was to foam at the mouth, but now the action of the sharp bit on my tongue and jaw, and the constrained position of my head and throat, always caused me to froth at the mouth more or less. Some people think it very fine to see this, and say, "What fine, spirited creatures!" But it is just as unnatural for horses as for men to foam at the mouth; it is a sure sign of some discomfort, and should be attended to. Besides this, there was a pressure on my windpipe, which often made my breathing very uncomfortable; when I returned from my work, my neck and chest were strained and painful, my mouth and tongue tender, and I felt worn and depressed.

In my old home I always knew that John and my master were my friends; but here, although in many ways I was well treated, I had no friend. York might have known, and very likely did know, how that rein harassed me; but I suppose he took it as a matter of course that could not be helped; at any rate, nothing was done to relieve me.

## Chapter XI A Horse Fair

No doubt a horse fair is a very amusing place to those who have nothing to lose; at any rate, there is plenty to see.

Long strings of young horses out of the country, fresh from the marshes, and droves of shaggy little Welsh ponies, no higher than Merrylegs; and hundreds of cart horses of all sorts, some of them with their long tails braided up and tied with scarlet cord; and a good many like myself, handsome and high-bred, but fallen into the middle class, through some accident or blemish, unsoundness of wind, or some other complaint. There were some splendid animals quite in their prime, and fit for anything, they were throwing out their legs and showing off their paces in high style, as they were trotted out with a leading rein, the groom running by the side. But round in the background there were a number of poor things, sadly broken down with hard work, with their knees knuckling over and their hind legs swinging out at every step; and there were some very dejected-looking old horses, with the under-lip hanging down and the ears lying back heavily, as if there was no more pleasure in life, and no more hope; there were some so thin you might see all their ribs, and some with old sores on their backs and hips. These were sad sights for a horse to look upon, who knows not but he may come to the same state. , I was put with some useful-looking horses, and a good many people came to look at us. The gentlemen always turned from me when they saw my broken knees; though the man who had me swore it was only a slip in the stall.

The first thing was to pull my mouth open, then to look at my eyes, then feel all the way down my legs and give me a hard feel of the skin and flesh, and then try my paces. It was wonderful what a difference there was in the way these things were done. Some did it in a rough, off-hand way, as if one was only a piece of wood; while others would take their hands gently over one's body, with a pat now and then, as much as to say, "By your leave." Of course, I judged a good deal of the buyers by their manners to myself.

## Anna Sewell

There was one man, I thought, if he would buy me, I should be happy. He was not a gentleman. He was rather a small man, but well made, and quick in all his motions. I knew in a moment, by the way he handled me, that he was used to horses; he spoke gently, and his gray eye had a kindly, cheery look in it. It may seem strange to say—but it is true all the same—that the clean, fresh smell there was about him made me take to him; no smell of old beer and tobacco, which I hated, but a fresh smell as if he had come out of a hayloft. He offered twenty-three pounds for me; but that was refused, and he walked away. I looked after him, but he was gone, and a very hard-looking, loud-voiced man came. I was dreadfully afraid he would have me; but he walked off. One or two more came who did not mean business. Then the hard-faced man came back again and offered twenty-three pounds. A very close bargain was being driven, for my salesman began to think he should not get all he asked, and must come down; but just then the gray-eyed man came back again. I could not help reaching out my head toward him. He stroked my face kindly. "Well, old chap," he said, "I think we should suit each other. I'll give twenty-four for him."

"Say twenty-five, and you shall have him." , "Twenty-four then," said my friend, in a very decided tone, "and not another sixpence—yes, or no?"

"Done," said the salesman; "and you may depend upon it there's a monstrous deal of quality in that horse, and if you want him for cab work he's a bargain."

The money was paid on the spot, and my new master took my halter, and led me out of the fair to an inn, where he had a saddle and bridle ready. He gave me a good feed of oats, and stood by while I ate it, talking to himself and talking to me. Half an hour after, we were on our way to London, through pleasant lanes and country roads, until we came into the great thoroughfare, on which we traveled steadily, till in the twilight we reached the great city. The gas lamps were already lighted; there were streets and streets crossing each other, for mile upon mile. I thought we should never come to the end of them. At last, in passing through one, we came to a long cab stand, when my rider called out in a cheery voice, "Good-night, Governor!"

"Hallo!" cried a voice. "Have you got a good one?"

"I think so," replied my owner.

"I wish you luck with him."

"Thank ye, Governor," and he rode on. We soon turned up one of the side-streets, and about half-way up that we turned into a very narrow street, with rather poor-looking houses on one side, and what seemed to be coach-houses and stables on the other.

My owner pulled up at one of the houses and whistled. The door flew open, and a young woman, followed by a little girl and boy, ran out. There was a very lively greeting as my rider dismounted. "Now, then, Harry, my boy, open the gates, and mother will bring us the lantern."

The next minute they were all round me in the stable yard. "Is he gentle, father?" "Yes, Dolly, as gentle as your own kitten; come and pat him." At once the little hand was patting about all over my shoulder without fear. How good it felt!

"Let me get him a bran mash while you rub him down," said the mother. "Do, Polly, it's just what he wants; and I know you've got a beautiful mash ready for me."

I was led into a comfortable, clean-smelling stall with plenty of dry straw, and after a capital supper, I lay down, thinking I was going to be happy.

## Chapter XII A London Cab Horse

My new master's name was Jeremiah Barker, but as every one called him Jerry, I shall do the same. Polly, his wife, was just as good a match as a man could have. She was a plump, trim, tidy little woman, with smooth, dark hair, dark eyes, and a merry little mouth. The boy was nearly twelve years old, a tall, frank, good-tempered lad; and little Dorothy (Dolly they called her) was her mother over again, at eight years old. They were all wonderfully fond of each other; I never knew such a happy, merry family before or since. Jerry had a cab of his own, and two horses, which he drove and attended to himself. His other horse was a tall, white, rather large-boned animal, called Captain. He was old now, but when he was young he must have been splendid; he had still a proud way of holding his head and arching his neck; in fact, he was a high-bred, fine-mannered, noble old horse, every inch of him. He told me that in his early youth he went to the Crimean War; he belonged to an officer in the cavalry, and used to lead the regiment.

The next morning, when I was well-groomed, Polly and Dolly came into the yard to see me and make friends. Harry had been helping his father since the early morning, and had stated his opinion that I should turn out "a regular brick." Polly brought me a slice of apple, and Dolly a piece of bread, and made as much of me as if I had been the Black Beauty of olden time. It was a great treat to be petted again and talked to in a gentle voice, and I let them see as well as I could that I wished to be friendly. Polly thought I was very handsome, and a great deal too good for a cab, if it was not for the broken knees.

"Of course there's no one to tell us whose fault that was," said Jerry, "and as long as I don't know I shall give him the benefit of the doubt; for a firmer, neater stepper I never rode. We'll call him Jack, after the old one—shall we, Polly?"

"Do," she said, "for I like to keep a good name going."

Captain went out in the cab all the morning. Harry came in after school to feed me and give me water. In the afternoon I was put into the cab. Jerry took as much pains to see if the collar and bridle fitted comfortably as if he had been John Manly over again. There was no check-rein, no curb, nothing but a plain ring snaffle. What a blessing that was!

After driving through the side-street we came to the large cabstand where Jerry had said "Good-night." On one side of this wide street were high houses with wonderful shop fronts, and on the other was an old church and churchyard, surrounded by iron palisades. Alongside these iron rails a number of cabs were drawn up, waiting for passengers; bits of hay were lying about on the ground; some of the men were standing together talking; some were sitting on their boxes reading the newspaper; and one or two were feeding their horses with bits of hay, and giving them a drink of water. We pulled up in the rank at the back of the last cab. Two or three men came round and began to look at me and pass their remarks.

"Very good for a funeral," said one.

"Too smart-looking," said another, shaking his head in a very wise way; "you'll find out something wrong one of these fine mornings, or my name isn't Jones."

"Well," said Jerry pleasantly, "I suppose I need not find it out till it find me out, eh? And if so, I'll keep up my spirits a little longer."

Then there came up a broad-faced man, dressed in a great gray coat with great gray capes and great white buttons, a gray hat, and a blue comforter loosely tied around his neck; his hair was gray, too; but he was a jolly-looking fellow, and the other men made way for him. He looked me all over, as if he had been going to buy me; and then straightening himself up with a grunt, he said, "He's the right sort for you, Jerry; I don't care what you gave for him, he'll be worth it." Thus my character was established on the stand. This man's name was Grant, but he was called "Gray Grant," or "Governor Grant." He had been the longest on that stand of any of the men, and he took it upon himself to settle matters and stop disputes.

The first week of my life as a cab horse was very trying. I had never been used to London, and the noise, the hurry, the crowds of horses, carts, and carriages, that I had to make my way through, made me feel anxious and harassed; but I soon found that I could ,perfectly trust my driver, and then I made myself easy, and got used to it.

Jerry was as good a driver as I had ever known; and what was better, he took as much thought for his horses as he did for himself. He soon found out that I was willing to work and do my best; and he never laid the whip on me, unless it was gently drawing the end of it over my back, when I was to go on; but generally I knew this quite well by the way in which he took up the reins; and I believe his whip was more frequently stuck up by his side than in his hand.

In a short time I and my master understood each other, as well as horse and man can do. In the stable, too, he did all that he could for our comfort. The stalls were the old-fashioned style, too much on the slope; but he had two movable bars fixed across the back of our stalls, so that at night, when we were resting, he just took off our halters and put up the bars, and thus we could turn about and stand whichever way we pleased, which is a great comfort.

Jerry kept us very clean, and gave us as much change of food as he could, and always plenty of it; and not only that, but he always gave us plenty of clean fresh water, which he allowed to stand by us both night and day, except of course when we came in warm. Some people say that a horse ought not to drink all he likes; but I know if we are allowed to drink when we want it we drink only a little at a time, and it does us a great deal more good than swallowing down half a bucketful at a time because we have been left without till we are thirsty and miserable. Some grooms will go home to their beer and leave us for hours with our dry hay and oats and nothing to moisten them; then of course we gulp down too much at once, which helps to spoil our breathing and sometimes chills our stomachs. But the best thing that we had here was our Sundays for rest! we worked so hard in the week, that I do not think we could have kept up to it, but for that day; besides, we had then time to enjoy each other's company.

## Chapter XIII Dolly And A Real Gentleman

The winter came in early, with a great deal of cold and wet. There was snow, or sleet, or rain, almost every day for weeks, changing only for keen driving winds or sharp frosts. The horses all felt it very much. When it is a dry cold, a couple of good thick rugs will keep the warmth in us; but when it is soaking rain, they soon get wet through and are no good. Some of the drivers had a waterproof cover to throw over, which was a fine thing; but some of the men were so poor that they could not protect either themselves or their horses, and many of them suffered very much that winter. When we horses had worked half the day we went to our dry stables, and could rest; while they had to sit on their boxes, sometimes staying out as late as one or two o'clock in the morning, if they had a party to wait for.

When the streets were slippery with frost or snow, that was the worst of all for us horses; one mile of such traveling with a weight to draw, and no firm footing, would take more out of us than four on a good road; every nerve and muscle of our bodies is on the strain to keep our balance; and, added to this, the fear of falling is more exhausting than anything else. If the roads are very bad, indeed, our shoes are roughed, but that makes us feel nervous at first.

One cold windy day, Dolly brought Jerry a basin of something hot, and was standing by him while he ate it. He had scarcely begun, when a gentleman, walking toward us very fast, held up his umbrella. Jerry touched his hat in return, gave the basin to Dolly, and was taking off my cloth, when the gentleman, hastening up, cried out, "No, no, finish your soup, my friend; I have not much time to spare, but I can wait till you have done, and set your little girl safe on the pavement."

So saying, he seated himself in the cab. Jerry thanked him kindly, and came back to Dolly. "There, Dolly, that's a gentleman; that's a real gentleman, Dolly; he has got time and thought for the comfort of a poor cabman and a little girl."

Jerry finished his soup, set the child across, and then took his orders to drive to Clapham Rise. Several times after that, the same gentleman took our cab. I think he was very fond of dogs and horses, for whenever we took him to his own door, two or three dogs would come bounding out to meet him. Sometimes he came round and patted me saying in his quiet, pleasant way: "This horse has got a good master, and he deserves it." It was a very rare thing for any one to notice the horse that had been working for him. I have known ladies to do it now and then, and this gentleman, and one or two others have given me a pat and a kind word; but ninety-nine out of a hundred would as soon think of patting the steam engine that drew the train.

One day, he and another gentleman took our cab; they stopped at a shop in R---- Street, and while his friend went in, he stood at the door. A little ahead of us on the other side of the street, a cart with two very fine horses was standing before some wine vaults; the carter was not with them, and I cannot tell how long they had been standing, but they seemed to think they had waited long enough, and began to move off. Before they had gone, many paces, the carter came running out and caught them. He seemed furious at their having moved, and with whip and rein punished them brutally, even beating them about the head. Our gentleman saw it all, and stepping quickly across the street, said in a decided voice: "If you don't stop that directly, I'll have you arrested for leaving your horses, and for brutal conduct."

The man, who had clearly been drinking, poured forth some abusive language, but he left off knocking the horses about, and taking the reins, got into his cart; meantime our friend had quietly taken a notebook from his pocket, and looking at the name and address painted on the cart, he wrote something down.

"What do you want with that?" growled the carter, as he cracked his whip and was moving on. A nod and a grim smile was the only answer he got.

On returning to the cab, our friend was joined by his companion, who said laughing, "I should have thought, Wright, you had enough business of your own to look after, without troubling yourself about other people's horses and servants."

Our friend stood still for a moment, and throwing his head a little back, "Do you know why this world is as bad as it is?"

"No," said the other.

"Then I'll tell you. It is because people think only about their own business, and won't trouble themselves to stand up for the oppressed, nor bring the wrong-doer to light. I never see a wicked thing like this without doing what I can, and many a master has thanked me for letting him know how his horses have been used."

"I wish there were more gentlemen like you, sir," said Jerry, "for they are wanted badly enough in this city."

## Chapter XIV Poor Ginger

One day, while our cab and many others were waiting outside one of the parks where music was playing, a shabby old cab drove up beside ours. The horse was an old worn-out chestnut, with an ill-kept coat, and bones that showed plainly through it, the knees knuckled over, and the fore-legs were very unsteady. I had been eating some hay, and the wind rolled a little lock of it that way, and the poor creature put out her long thin neck and picked it up, and then turned round and looked about for more. There was a hopeless look in the dull eye that I could not help noticing, and then, as I was thinking where I had seen that horse before, she looked full at me and said, "Black Beauty, is that you?"

It was Ginger! but how changed! The beautifully arched and glossy neck was now straight, and lank, and fallen in; the clean, straight legs and delicate fetlocks were swelled; the joints were grown out of shape with hard work; the face, that was once so full of spirit and life, was now full of suffering, and I could tell by the heaving of her sides, and her frequent cough, how bad her breath was. , Our drivers were standing together a little way off, so I sidled up to her a step or two, that we might have a little quiet talk. It was a sad tale that she had to tell.

After a twelvemonth's run off at Earlshall, she was considered to be fit for work again, and was sold to a gentleman. For a little while she got on very well, but after a longer gallop than usual, the old strain returned, and after being rested and doctored she was again sold. In this way she changed hands several times, but always getting lower down.

"And so at last," said she, "I was bought by a man who keeps a number of cabs and horses, and lets them out. You look well off, and I am glad of it, but I could not tell you what my life has been. When they found out my weakness, they said I was not worth what they gave for me, and that I must go into one of the low cabs, and just be used up; that is what they are doing, whipping and working with never one thought of what I suffer—they paid for me, and must get it out of me, they say. The man who hires me now pays a deal of money to the owner every day, and so he has to get it out of me, too; and so it's all the week round and round, with never a Sunday rest."

I said, "You used to stand up for yourself if you were ill-used."

"Ah!" she said, "I did once, but it's no use; men are strongest, and if they are cruel and have no feeling, there is nothing that we can do but just bear it—bear it on and on to the end. I wish the end was come, I wish I was dead. I have seen dead horses, and I am sure they do not suffer pain."

I was very much troubled, and I put my nose up to hers, but I could say nothing to comfort her. I think she was pleased to see me, for she said, "You are the only friend I ever had."

Just then her driver came up, and with a tug at her mouth, backed her out of the line and drove off, leaving me very sad, indeed.

A short time after this, a cart with a dead horse in it passed our cab stand. The head hung out of the cart tail, the lifeless tongue was slowly dropping with blood; and the sunken eyes! but I can't speak of them, the sight was too dreadful! It was a chestnut horse with a long, thin neck. I saw a white streak down the forehead. I believe it was Ginger; I hoped it was, for then her troubles would be over. Oh! if men were more merciful, they would shoot us before we came to such misery.

## Chapter XV

At a sale I found myself in company with a lot of horses—some lame, some broken-winded, some old, and some that I am sure it would have been merciful to shoot.

The buyers and sellers, too, many of them, looked not much better off than the poor beasts they were bargaining about. There were poor old men, trying to get a horse or pony for a few pounds, that might drag about some little wood or coal cart. There were poor men trying to sell a worn-out beast for two or three pounds, rather than have the greater loss of killing him. Some of them looked as if poverty and hard times had hardened them all over; but there were others that I would have willingly used the last of my strength in serving; poor and shabby, but kind and humane, with voices that I could trust. There was one tottering old man that took a great fancy to me, and I to him, but I was not strong enough—it was an anxious time! Coming from the better part of the fair, I noticed a man who looked like a gentleman farmer, with a young boy by his side; he had a broad back and round shoulders, a kind, ruddy face, and he wore a broad-brimmed hat. When he came up to me and my companions, he stood still, and gave a pitiful look round upon us. I saw his eye rest on me; I had still a good mane and tail, which did something for my appearance. I pricked my ears and looked at him.

"There's a horse, Willie, that has known better days."

"Poor old fellow!" said the boy; "do you think, grandpapa, he was ever a carriage horse?"

"Oh, yes! my boy," said the farmer, coming closer, "he might have been anything when he was young; look at his nostrils and his ears, the shape of his neck and shoulder; there's a deal of breeding about that horse." He put out his hand and gave me a kind pat on the neck. I put out my nose in answer to his kindness; the boy stroked my face.

"Poor old fellow! see, grandpapa, how well he understands kindness. Could not you buy him and make him young again as you did with Ladybird?"

"My dear boy, I can't make all old horses young; besides, Ladybird was not so very old, as she was run down and badly used."

"Well, grandpapa, I don't believe that this one is old; look at his mane and tail. I wish you would look into his mouth, and then you could tell; though he is so very thin, his eyes are not sunk like some old horses." The old gentleman laughed. "Bless the boy! he is as horsey as his old grandfather."

"But do look at his mouth, grandpapa, and ask the price; I am sure he would grow young in our meadows."

The man who had brought me for sale now put in his word. "The young gentleman's a real knowing one, sir. Now, the fact is, this 'ere hoss is just pulled down with over-work in the cabs; he's not an old one, and I heard as how the vetenary said that a six-months' run off would set him right up, being as how his wind was not broken. I've had the tending of him these ten days past, and a gratefuller, pleasanter animal I never met with, and 'twould be worth a gentleman's while to give a five-pound note for him, and let him have a chance. I'll be bound he'd be worth twenty pounds next spring."

The old gentleman laughed, and the little boy looked up eagerly. "O, grandpapa, did you not say the colt sold for five pounds more than you expected? You would not be poorer if you did buy this one."

The farmer slowly felt my legs, which were much swelled and strained; then he looked at my mouth. "Thirteen or fourteen, I should say; just trot him out, will you?"

I arched my poor thin neck, raised my tail a little and threw out my legs as well as I could, for they were very stiff.

"What is the lowest you will take for him?" said the farmer as I came back. "Five pounds, sir; that was the lowest price my master set."

"'Tis a speculation," said the old gentleman, shaking his head, but at the same time slowly drawing out his purse, "quite a speculation! Have you any more business here?" he said, counting the sovereigns into his hand. "No, sir, I can take him for you to the inn, if you please."

"Do so, I am now going there."

## Chapter XVI My Last Home

One day, during this summer, the groom cleaned and dressed me with such extraordinary care that I thought some new change must be at hand; he trimmed my fetlocks and legs, passed the tar-brush over my hoofs, and even parted my forelock. I think the harness had an extra polish. Willie seemed half-anxious, half-merry, as he got into the chaise with his grandfather. "If the ladies take to him," said the old gentleman, "they'll be suited and he'll be suited; we can but try."

At the distance of a mile or two from the village, we came to a pretty, low house, with a lawn and shrubbery at the front, and a drive up to the door. Willie rang the bell, and asked if Miss Blomefield or Miss Ellen was at home. Yes, they were. So, while Willie stayed with me, Mr. Thoroughgood went into the house. In about ten minutes he returned, followed by three ladies; one tall, pale lady, wrapped in a white shawl, leaned on a younger lady, with dark eyes and a merry face; the other, a very stately-looking person, was Miss Blomefield. They all came and looked at me and asked questions. The younger lady—that was Miss Ellen—took to me very much; she said she was sure she should like me, I had such a good face. The tall, pale lady said she should always be nervous in riding, behind a horse that had once been down, as I might come down again, and if I did she should never get over the fright."

## Anna Sewell

"You see, ladies," said Mr. Thoroughgood, "many first-rate horses have had their knees broken through the carelessness of their drivers, without any fault of their own, and from what I see of this horse, I should say that is his case; but, of course, I do not wish to influence you. If you incline, you can have him on trial, and then your coachman will see what he thinks of him."

"You have always been such a good adviser to us about our horses," said the stately lady, "that your recommendation would go a long way with me, and if my sister Lavinia sees no objection, we will accept your offer of a trial, with thanks."

It was then arranged that I should be sent for the next day. In the morning a smart-looking young man came for me; at first, he looked pleased; but when he saw my knees, he said in a disappointed voice: "I didn't think, sir, you would have recommended a blemished horse like that."

"'Handsome is that handsome does,'" said my master; "you are only taking him on trial, and I am sure you will do fairly by him, young man; if he is not safe as any horse you ever drove, send him back."

I was led to my new home, placed in a comfortable stable, fed, and left to myself. The next day, when my groom was cleaning my face, he said: "That is just like the star that Black Beauty had, he is much the same height, too; I wonder where he is now."

A little further on, he came to the place in my neck where I was bled, and where a little knot was left in the skin. He almost started, and begun to look me over carefully, talking to himself. "White star in the forehead, one white foot on the off side, this little knot just in that place"; then, looking at the middle of my back—"and as I am alive, there is that little patch of white hair that John used to call 'Beauty's threepenny bit.' It must be Black Beauty! Why,, Beauty! Beauty! do you know me? little Joe Green, that almost killed you?" And he began patting and patting me as if he was quite overjoyed.

I could not say that I remembered him, for now he was a fine grown young fellow, with black whiskers, and a man's voice, but I was sure he knew me, and that he was Joe Green, and I was very glad.

I put my nose up to him, and tried to say that we were friends. I never saw a man so pleased.

"Give you a fair trial! I should think so, indeed! I wonder who the rascal was that broke your knees, my old Beauty! you must have been badly served out somewhere; well, well, it won't be my fault if you haven't good times of it now. I wish John Manly was here to see you."

In the afternoon I was put into a low Park chair and brought to the door. Miss Ellen was going to try me, and Green went with her. I soon found that she was a good driver, and she seemed pleased with my paces. I heard Joe telling her about me, and that he was sure I was Squire Gordon's old "Black Beauty."

When we returned, the other sisters came out to hear how I had behaved myself. She told them what she had just heard, and said: "I shall certainly write to Mrs. Gordon, and tell her that her favorite horse has come to us. How pleased she will be!"

After this I was driven every day for a week or so, and as I appeared to be quite safe, Miss Lavinia at last ventured out in the small close carriage. After this it was quite decided to keep me and call me by my old name of Black Beauty.

I have now lived in this happy place a whole year.

Printed in Great Britain
by Amazon